For Jordan,
who has always run the show —C. R. S.

For Mom,
who encouraged me to write —R. J. G.

For Emmy and Kay,
who taught me the importance of working together —K. Y.

ATHENEUM BOOKS FOR YOUNG READERS · An imprint of Simon & Schuster Children's Publishing Division · 1230 Avenue of the Americas, New York, New York 10020 · Text copyright © 2015 by Corey Rosen Schwartz and Rebecca J. Gomez · Illustrations copyright © 2015 by Keika Yamaguchi · All rights reserved, including the right of reproduction in whole or in part in any form. · ATHENEUM BOOKS FOR YOUNG READERS is a registered trademark of Simon & Schuster, Inc. · Atheneum logo is a trademark of Simon & Schuster, Inc. · For information about special discounts for bulk purchases, please contact Simon & Schuster Special Sales at 1-866-506-1949 or business@simonandschuster.com. · The Simon & Schuster Speakers Bureau can bring authors to your live event. For more information or to book an event, contact the Simon & Schuster Speakers Bureau at 1-866-248-3049 or visit our website at www.simonspeakers.com. · Book design by Lauren Rille · The text for this book is set in Yourz Truly. · The illustrations for this book are rendered digitally. · Manufactured in China · 0315 SCP · First Edition · 10 9 8 7 6 5 4 3 2 1 · Library of Congress Cataloging-in-Publication Data · Schwartz, Corey Rosen, author. · What about Moose? / by Corey Rosen Schwartz and Rebecca J. Gomez ; illustrated by Keika Yamaguchi. — 1st ed. · p. cm. · Summary: "Fox and her friends are building a playhouse. Everything goes smoothly until bossy Moose tromps in and tries to be in charge of everything. When Moose's bossing causes the project to go awry, can the friends work as a team to come up with a solution?"— Provided by publisher. · ISBN 978-1-4814-0496-9 (hardcover) · ISBN 978-1-4814-0497-6 (eBook) · [1. Stories in rhyme. 2. Building—Fiction. 3. Bossiness—Fiction. 4. Moose—Fiction. 5. Animals—Fiction] I. Gomez, Rebecca J., author. II. Yamaguchi, Keika, illustrator. III. Title. · PZ8.3.S38927Wh 2015 · [E]—dc23 2013041941

By Corey Rosen Schwartz & Rebecca J. Gomez

WHAT ABOUT MOOSE?

Illustrated by Keika Yamaguchi

Atheneum Books for Young Readers · New York   London   Toronto   Sydney   New Delhi

Fox met her friends, with her toolbox in hand.
"Time to start building! Now, here's what I've planned."
She divvied up jobs, and then Moose trotted in.

"I'M HERE," he announced.
"Let construction begin!"

He put on a hard hat and said,
"Let's get to it.

"I'll be the foreman.
I know how to do it!"

"Now, hold on," said Fox.
"Let's work as a team.
We need you to help
with that big heavy beam."

But Moose made a sign that said "Caution: Work Zone" and shouted commands from a big megaphone.

"Bear, crank the handle to tighten that brace.

"Toad, keep on sanding, but pick up the pace."

"But what about you, Moose?" Toad asked with concern.

"I'm overseeing,"
said Moose, looking stern.

He spotted and jotted down
all imperfections,
while marching around
doing careful inspections.

"Skunk, put your back
into lifting those poles!

"Porcupine, watch it!
You're poking small holes."

He spouted and shouted all kinds of advice.

"Measure correctly!
We must be precise."

"But what about you, Moose?" Fox asked with a glare.
"You're tromping about but not doing your share."

Moose wiped his forehead. "I've worked up a sweat!
Being in charge is the toughest job yet."

Skunk nailed the crossbeams to make the floor strong,
but Moose said . . .

"Not that way.
You're doing it wrong.
The floor and the door
should be just
a bit straighter."

Then Porcupine mumbled, "Who made *him* dictator?"

Fox laid the floorboards as Toad manned the drill.
Bear did the caulking with handyman skill.

Moose clambered up as they nailed the planks tight.

"Time for the walls," he said. "Don't take all night!"

"But what about you, Moose?
You're in the way."

"Nonsense," said Moose. "Just do as I say."

A clunkety-plunk. One wall was complete.
"Perfect!" said Moose. "But watch out for my feet."

The walls all went up
as they hefted
and pounded . . .

. . . and built around Moose until he was surrounded.
"Get ready! Now, steady . . . now listen to me.
Lift up the roof when I count one-two-three."

"But what about YOU, Moose?"
the friends said as one.

Moose said, "No questions!
Our work's almost done.

"Don't worry—just hurry
and set it on top."

They put it in place
with a loud, banging

plop!

And it was too late when Moose hollered,

"STOP!"

"Hey, what about *me*?"
Moose's muffled voice cried.

"You built all around me. Now I'm shut inside.
I'll never squeeze out of this tiny front door!
What are you all just standing there for?"

Bear tried to pull using all of his might.

"It's hopeless!" cried Moose.

"This doorway's too tight."

He groaned and he grumbled. "It's squishing my butt!"
"We'll help you," said Fox, "if you keep your mouth shut!"

"So, here's my idea." And they all huddled near,

plotting and planning, so Moose couldn't hear.

With thumping and bumping, they worked around Moose,
and soon they were ready to set their friend loose.

A push and a smush,
and he popped back inside.

"Oh wow!
A trapdoor!"

He zipped down the slide.

Then Fox named a game
that the friends could all play.

And what about Moose?

He played it—their way!

Follow
the leader!

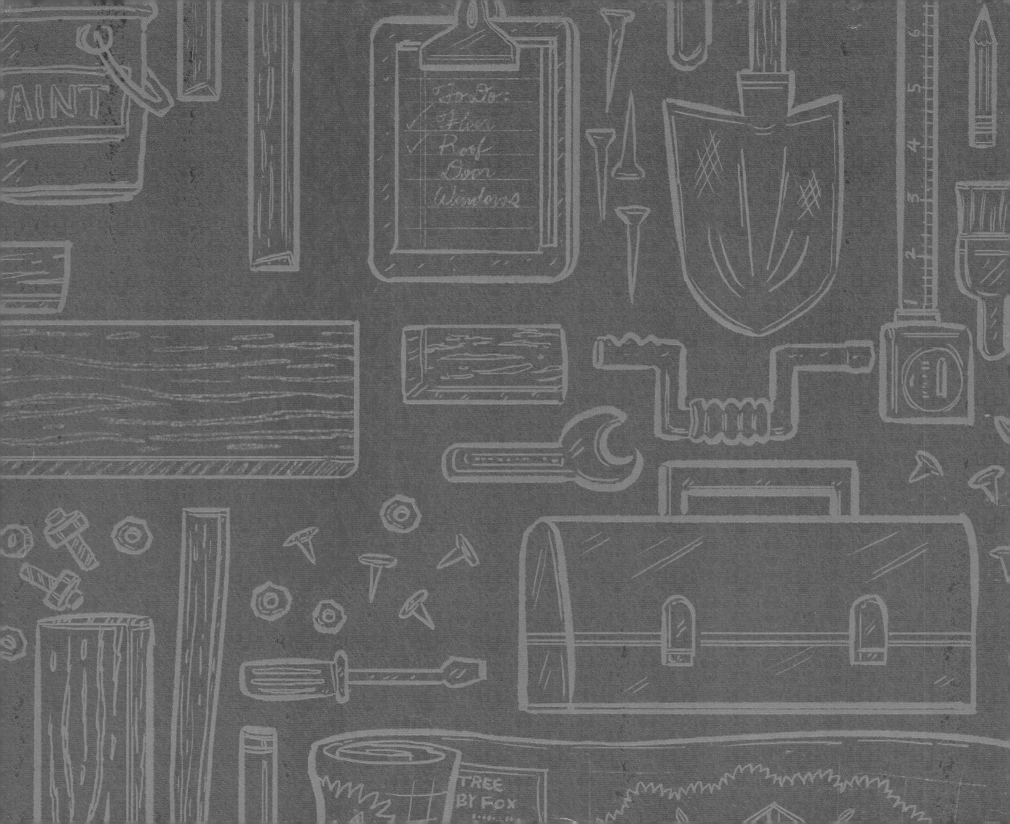